The Ghost of Etiquette

Beth Webster

Also by Beth Webster,
Ghosts Are Only Human, From the Files of Richard West,
(sequel to *The Ghost of Etiquette.*)
My Poems
A California Fairy Tale
Just for Fun, Let's Draw Cats

1

The Ghost of Etiquette

Contents

Introduction

Welcome, Dear Reader, and thank you for being here. I'm afraid I'm not the world's best storyteller. An unreliable narrator, they'll call me, maybe. The thing is, I'm the only one who really knows this story, and I feel I have to tell somebody. It's about my friend, Amy Vanderbilt. She was a brilliant writer, an etiquette expert and a fine cook. She was also very kind. Some say the lady killed herself. I know she did not.

My name is Beth Jones. I live with my husband, Parker, in a small old California bungalow full of old furniture, in a lush and shady neighborhood of bigger, old homes. Parker and I have both spent our lives working very hard and making very little money. Now Parker is unemployed, and I make coasters and sell them online for a living. We get by on next to nothing. We don't even own a cell phone, but we do have a computer.

In short, Dear Reader, we are nobodies. Thus, we might seem unlikely hosts for such a lady as Miss Vanderbilt, who was described as elegant and cosmopolitan and who lived on the East coast, among the upper crustaceans. I'm not sure when or why we met Miss Vanderbilt. I guess it all began with an invitation...

CHAPTER ONE

Parker was standing at the door with my old pink Sear's suitcase, bellowing, over and over, "This is it. You're not going to see me again. You'd better be sure you want me to leave." Then we heard footsteps on the porch. Parker stopped yelling.

I went across the room and opened the suitcase. I wanted to see what was in there. I found pajamas, t-shirts, about a million socks.

"Be careful. There's a ..." Parker said, as a miner's pick dropped from a pair of rolled-up jeans.

I said, "Why are you taking *my* suitcase?"

"The handle's broken on mine," Parker shouted. Then the screen door creaked loudly, and the mail shot through the slot and hit the floor with a smack. Parker picked up the envelopes, flipped through them, and tossed me something.

I opened it and found an invitation to a local reception for a former professor who'd just become Poet Laureate of the United States.

"This is big," Parker said. "You have to go."

"Yes," I said, but I wasn't certain.

Parker, per usual, was panicking. "I don't know what to wear. I don't know which fork to use. I don't even know how to act at an event like that."

"I know," I said. Truthfully, I felt the same way. I went over to the bookshelf and picked up a dusty old copy of Amy Vanderbilt's hefty book on the social graces. I handed it to Parker, who opened it at random, sank into a chair, and became quickly absorbed.

After that, Parker was quiet for a change. I did stuff around the house.   Parker spent the rest of the day right there in the chair, silently reading, which was fine with me. I wondered what was so fascinating in those pages.

Later that night, I went to draw a bath and found Parker, who hardly ever cries, in the bathroom, crying. This surprised me.

I turned on the tap. "What's wrong?" I asked.

Our eyes met in the mirror. Parker said, "I want you to remember me." He turned back to the mirror and sighed. "My face..." he said.

I said, "Your face is fine. It's your mind I would switch if I could."

Parker smiled as if this were a compliment.

I got into the bath.

"May I join you?" Parker asked.

"Of course," I said.

The air was cold, and steam rose from the bath water and swirled around us like a veil.

CHAPTER TWO

The next morning, Parker, who had taken quite a liking to the words of Amy Vanderbilt, was gliding all around the place, speaking in a woman's voice, calling me "my love" or better yet, calling me by my name, with a sweet lilt that touched me inside. I hardly recognized this Parker, whose voice and body language were relaxed and free of defensiveness and hostility.

"This coffee is wonderful," Parker said.

I said, "It's the same coffee we always have."

I had a nervous and excited feeling, as if we were having company. While Parker sat on the sofa, sipping black coffee as if he hadn't had any for forty years, I swept and mopped the hardwood floors. I replaced the dusty candles in the sconces on the walls, then lit the wicks and blew them out. I cleaned the whole house.

The next day, Parker was still in a good mood. This was very strange.

"Have you decided what you are wearing to the reception?" Parker asked.

"I don't think I'm going. I don't have anything to wear," I said. Except for trips to the grocery store, I hadn't been out of the house for a year.

Now, Parker was opening drawers and looking in the

closet, saying, "I'm sure we can find a pretty dress. It really is an honor to be invited."

"No one will miss me," I said.

"Someone thought to invite you, an old friend, maybe," Parker said. He reached into the closet, pulled out a black velvet and held it up to my shoulders.

I knew this was an important event. I knew that I had to attend, out of respect for my professor.

See, I used to hang out with an academic crowd, poets, professors and writers. They would all be at the upcoming event. I hadn't seen my friends for several years. Every time I tried to attend a reading or a party, Parker somehow found a way to stop me. Whenever we went out of the house, he found a way to start a scene in public. I didn't like it. I stopped going out of the house, and then I got used to it.

Dear Reader, please allow me to explain a few things. See Parker was full of anger from the day we met. I used to think that I could cure that ailment. Conflict has always made me uncomfortable. For most of my life, I managed to avoid it. Parker, however, thrived on turmoil and had an endless endurance for fighting. Something, it seemed, was always under his skin. Every email Parker sent was written in all caps and littered with exclamation points, and his phone calls always ended with a slam. My son Evan moved out at seventeen because he didn't like to hear Parker shouting all the time. "Old Yeller," Evan called Parker. Parker claimed that a man should be allowed to yell in his own home. He called it "venting." When I pointed out that he would be fired at work for yelling the way he did, he said,

"Everyone has two personalities: one for work and one for home."

Amy Vanderbilt said, "One face to the world, another at home, makes for misery." When I pointed this out to Parker, he just yelled at me.

In her Complete Book of Etiquette, Amy Vanderbilt said, "An angry tone is catching." Dear Reader, I had found this to be true. Before I met Parker, I'd always considered myself patient and good. Perhaps I had too much pride.

Maybe I had just never been tested. I'd changed a lot since meeting Parker, and not for the better.

Apparently, though, I wasn't the only one who could change. Lately, Parker had been nice part of the time, and I couldn't help wondering why...

CHAPTER THREE

I leaned my rake against a tree and watched Parker, curiously. See, usually he walked with a fast determined strut, hands balled into fists and a countenance to match-- pursed lips and an angry brow. Now Parker looked soft and vulnerable, weaving about the backyard, one wrist delicately bent, as if to keep an invisible bracelet from slipping over the hand.

"Hmm," I said. I watched Parker pick up a stick and gently free a butterfly from a spider's web. Something's changed, I thought.

That night, I noticed that Parker had begun to look at me when we were talking, instead of staring angrily into space. Then the strangest thing of all happened: I looked at my husband, and I saw another pair of eyes, set like jewels in his face. He sat up straight, with his hands folded neatly in his lap. His body looked the same, but in the smile, in the posture, I saw a different person. I couldn't stop staring. The anger that seemed to always simmer under the surface had dissipated somehow. The soul occupying Parker's body seemed peaceful and kind. I looked at my spouse, and I saw someone else on my couch.

Hmm, I said to myself, and I went and riffled through Parker's drawers, looking for drugs.

I watched out the window while Parker went to the corner and back for a paper. When he walked in the door, I said, "Have you been drinking?" and I sniffed his breath. He only laughed. He didn't get mad.

Now I started observing every nuance. I even took notes. I wrote. "Parker has acquired a certain elegance of movement." A day later, I scrawled, "He walks into walls and trips over the coffee table, then seems surprised when it hurts." Very odd, it seemed. How could someone become more poised and yet more clumsy at the same time?

Maybe it's another woman, I thought. Maybe Parker's in love. People do act funny when they are in love.

Parker said, "I'm going to water the fruit trees," and stepped out. I stood behind the front door and peeped through the peephole.

The mail carrier strolled up. She handed Parker the mail. "How's your team doing?" she asked. Then she laughed. Parker's team was doing terribly.

"Very well, thank you," Parker said, and then he turned around and walked back into the house. I had to jump back to keep from being hit by the door.

How odd, I thought. See, Parker was usually overly-friendly to women in such situations, always insisting on assisting them, always engaging them in long conversations.

The next day, Parker was still behaving strangely--being sweet to me. Maybe it's that book, I thought, and I went looking for Amy Vanderbilt's book. I found it on

Parker's nightstand. I opened it and perused its contents. Outside, rain was coming down in sheets. It was the perfect day for a good book. I got into bed with this one, and I read for hours. I found great wisdom and humor, sprinkled between the rules of polite behavior. I found a voice that was entertaining, even when describing the mundane details of entertaining.

That night, everything was quiet. I thought Parker had left me, because I couldn't hear the TV. I went into the living room to return Amy Vanderbilt's book to its shelf and found Parker there, shining like the moon in the blue light of winter dusk.

I said, "I didn't know you were here."

Parker said softly, "You have a nice library," as if seeing, for the first time, our hundreds of books.

I said, "Well, you know... English major."

The next morning I wrote in my notebook, "Parker seems uncomfortable in the usual clothes." He had stopped wearing shirts with sports team mantras and beer jokes. He would look through the drawers, take things out, neatly refold them, and put them back, before settling on something basic.

I worked on my coasters in peace for a while. Usually, Parker would stand in front of me, shouting about something while I worked.

I went to refill my coffee. It was an unseasonably

warm day. The kitchen was filled with sunlight. My mouth
dropped open when Parker emerged from the hallway,
wearing a filmy white dress and a pair of ballet slippers.

Something occurred to me then. I wondered if Parker
was acting the part of Amy Vanderbilt. Parker had, after all,
been a little obsessed with her lately. Yes, that's it, I thought.
I examined my notes:

> Parker wiped fingers on napkin instead of socks,
> started laughing at my jokes,
> started being sweet to me
> > stopped sitting around in underwear,
> quit mixing entire dinner into a pile before eating it,
> used the term "predicate nominative" in a sentence,
> is very sensitive lately,

Then something even stranger occurred to me.
Perhaps Parker wasn't acting. Suppose the ghost of Amy
Vanderbilt had taken up residence in Parker's body. Now
what? I thought. Since I couldn't know for certain, I decided
to run with that theory. And the evidence was quite
convincing.

For one thing, Parker didn't know the lyrics to
anything, or so I thought. Then one evening I heard the
unmistakable crackling of a phonograph record. I went into
the living room. "Night and Day" was emanating from the
old console, which had been meticulously dusted. Parker sat
neatly in a white wingback chair, singing every verse, with
the voice of an angel.

Did I mention that Parker couldn't carry a tune, was practically tone deaf in the past? "Any old note will do," I used to say, when Parker would start singing at Christmas parties and throw everyone off key.

Maybe, I thought, that's the reason Parker keeps bumping into the furniture and walking into walls. What would happen if a ghost, accustomed to walking right through walls and solid objects, decided to occupy a physical body? Wouldn't that ghost have to adjust to a world of solid objects? It was enough to make my brain spin.

Then, Parker started cooking and baking and doing it well. "So?" you might say. Well, for the past ten years, I had done all of the cooking. A few times, when we were having company, I asked Parker for help with the cooking, but he just stood there and ate all the ingredients as quickly as I could chop or measure them.

Parker loved to eat, but he hated to cook. I didn't mind, though, because he washed the dishes after every meal. He was adamant about it. Whenever I offered to do the dishes, Parker would become irritated and yell, "You know I do the dishes after every meal. I don't know why you even offer. I wash the dishes because you do all of the cooking. I don't know why you even ask. You cook. I do dishes. That's the way it is."

That was the old Parker. The new Parker cooked with me, side by side. The new Parker would head into the kitchen in the morning, make coffee and start the bread.

This Parker kneaded dough with a sensual shimmy and a soft smile.

This time, when I offered to do the dishes, Parker said, in that other voice, "You may rinse them, if you'd like," so we worked together, side by side, in quiet symmetry.

Parker said, "Don't you remember we always used to do them this way?"

"No," I said, because I didn't remember.

"I'm going to bake a cherry pie," Parker said one day.

I said, "My favorite," and I was quite excited. I hadn't had cherry pie in years.

We went into the kitchen, and Parker took some cherries from the freezer and set them out to thaw. Then he mixed up some dough, shaped it into a ball, cut it in half, and put it in the refrigerator.

When the dough was cold, Parker took a rolling pin and lightly rolled out one half. Then with one smooth motion, he flipped it into a glass dish. The dough settled into the dish, like magic, forming a perfect shell. Parker poked it with a fork. Then he stirred some sugar and sundry ingredients into the bowl of cherries and poured it into the shell. I sat in the breakfast nook and watched. Parker rolled out the rest of the pastry dough, covered the pie, pinched the edges lightly and poked the top with a fork, making holes in the shape of a heart. I was amazed. I knew the making of a pastry shell was a skill that took a lot of practice.

I also knew that Parker had never baked a pie in his life.

"Hmm," I said.

Forty minutes later, when the bell rang, Parker took the pie out of the oven and set it on the cooling rack. Some of the filling had come through the holes, making the outline of a heart. Now here's the strange part: the crust was rising and falling in the center, so that the heart appeared to be beating. I watched in amazement. I tried to come up with a scientific explanation. That's just pressure being released, I told myself. Physics can explain that.

Parker only smiled.

That evening, when the pie had finally cooled, I cut two slices. The filling didn't fall out the way it always did whenever I tried to make a pie. Then we tasted it, and it tasted like pie from heaven.

I felt a drop in my heart rate and blood pressure, hanging out with the new Parker. We laughed a lot together. The old Parker had a fine laugh, though I seldom heard it. The new Parker's laugh was just different, sudden, low and sincere, followed by a smile that lingered in the eyes.

Speaking of the eyes, where the old Parker always seemed to look past me, seemed to be in a hurry to get away from me, this one gazed at me so intently that, at first, it almost frightened me.

Sitting on the couch, after cherry pie and coffee, Parker looked me in the eyes and smiled with an expression so passionate and so sweet, I thought it must be love.

"Stop it," I said, though I meant the opposite, and the expression faded.

Every time I awoke that night, I found Parker holding me very tightly, so tightly that I had to pull away at first. Then I let go of my fear, and I began to need that love.

This might be a happily ever after story, but for one thing: at times, the old raised-by-wolves Parker would return, along with the sharp tone, the wild angry gestures. I was mystified.

CHAPTER FOUR

One morning, I was in the kitchen about to make breakfast, when the phone rang. I turned on the speakerphone. (The receiver was broken, so we always used the speaker.)

A voice said, "I bought some of your coasters. I was wondering if you do special orders."

"Yes," I said. "What is it?

Parker walked in, poured a bunch of granola into a stainless steel bowl, and stood beside me, crunching into the speaker phone.

"I have a company logo..." the customer said.

I motioned at Parker to crunch somewhere else. He gave me mean looks and kept on eating.

At the end of the call, I said, "Thank you very much," and hung up. Then I turned to Parker. "Why do you always do that?" I said.

"Do what?" Parker said.

The phone rang again. It was Evan. "I'm stopping by this weekend, is that okay?" he said.

I looked at Parker, who was clanging the spoon against

the bottom of the bowl, to get the last bit of cereal.

"Well?" I said. Parker just went on crunching.

"Yes," I said to Evan, "Of course. That's fine."

"What's all that crunching and clinking?" Evan said. "Why are you always crunching and clinking on the speaker-phone?"

"It's not me," I said. I looked at Parker, and I wondered where the ghost had gone.

By then, you see, I believed in the ghost. I had plenty of evidence for her existence. For instance, in the kitchen, the spices sometimes slid toward my hand when I reached for them. Book pages turned themselves. Lights flickered when I spoke to the ghost, and a little spark of light often twinkled and hovered in the air. When the spark was there, I could feel the ghost near.

It may sound strange, but these things helped me. Even when I was alone, I somehow felt less lonely. I had a friend to keep me company.

I began to miss the ghost whenever she was gone. Questions about her occupied my mind. I wondered if she remembered the details of her former life. I worried that she might be cold, without body heat. I wondered how thoughts could travel without the spark of neurons across the gray matter of a brain.

Was the ghost between worlds? Was she lost? I wanted to ask, but the words wouldn't come out. Perhaps I was afraid that I might frighten her away or that the spell would be broken if I came right out and said, "Are you for real?" I was also worried that Parker would call me crazy or use my words against me. I decided to wait and see what happened next.

CHAPTER FIVE

Four years ago, Parker decided to stop working and attend a two year vocational program at the college down the street. "They said at the orientation that we won't have time to do household chores, and we're not supposed to work," Parker announced. "You don't have to worry, though, because I've found you two extra jobs. You're going to teach remedial English from seven to nine weekday mornings and work at Chicken Pie Hut on Friday nights." This was all in addition to my usual job, serving banquets at The Pumpkin Coach.

Parker was forty-two at the time, and I was thirty-nine. I wasn't in the mood for self-sacrifice. I said, "Forget that. If that's what you want to do, go live somewhere else."

But Parker stayed. I worked three part-time jobs that year. Plus, in order to teach at the college, I had to go back to the Master's of Fine Arts program at the university. That year, Parker only came home at night and was too busy studying to talk to me or help out with the household chores. I enjoyed going back to school, and I liked teaching. Still, I was lonely, and I had trouble keeping up with laundry. Meanwhile, Parker was happy in a class full of women. When they called for help with homework late at night, he pretended to be the victim of mean witch, thus gaining their sympathy. My teenage son went to live with his father that year, because Parker always found time to yell at him. Through it all, Parker somehow kept everyone convinced that I was a controlling shrew.

My teaching job ended after four semesters, when I could no longer afford graduate school tuition on an adjunct's stipend. Parker never finished his vocational program.

For four years, I'd been begging Parker to move out, to no avail. Why would he leave a cozy little rent-free bungalow?

"I'll leave when you leave," Parker often said, which infuriated me, because I had bought the house long before I met Parker, and it was my home.

When "I'll leave when you leave," wore out, Parker started saying, "I'm going to Arizona, alone, to search for gold and precious stones in the desert with a mule. That's what I'm going to do." (Parker had cousins in Arizona who had offered "a place to escape" from me.)

For a long time, I'd been certain that Parker was only using me. I wondered if the ghost had come to save me. Then I wondered if I was close to death. After all, I had frequent chest pain, bad headaches, and no health insurance. Maybe I can talk to ghosts because I am on the brink of death, I thought, and I worried about that for a while.

CHAPTER SIX

I was in the bathroom, brushing my hair. Parker was in there too, cleaning the tub, which is something I usually did. I thought how stagnant and pathetic Parker's life must be. I refused to go anywhere, and Parker wouldn't leave, perhaps out of fear of being locked out of the house. I said, "Do you often get tired of me? Don't you want to get out of here and get away for a while?"

"No," Parker said. He stopped scrubbing and turned around to look at me in the mirror. He said, "I don't want to be away from you. You're my best friend."

"Hmm," I said. He looked so vulnerable, feminine, even.

"Of course you're my best friend. Don't you know that?" Parker said.

"No, I never knew that," I said. "I thought you saw me as your opponent, the other team, the enemy with whom you shared a bed and bungalow. You've called me bad names. You've called me a lot of things, but you've never called me your friend."

"I'm sorry," Parker said.

On the weekend, my son Evan, a science major, came to visit. He sat in the breakfast nook, watching Parker make a pie. While the two of them chatted politely about current events, Parker took a rolling pin and lightly rolled out a ball of dough, then with that one deft, delicate motion, flipped it into a pie pan. Like magic, it turned into a pie shell.

"You made that look easy," Evan said.

Parker only smiled.

After a while, when Parker stepped out the back door to get eggs from the chicken coop, Evan said, "Hey Mom, what's going on around here? Old Yeller is being nice. What's that all about?"

I said, "Your step-nut is channeling the ghost of Amy Vanderbilt."

Evan looked out the window, narrowed his eyes thoughtfully, and nodded. He wasn't one to believe in such things, but he seemed to accept my theory.

We watched Parker sashay across the backyard, followed by a flock of four friendly chickens.

"Non sequitur," Evan said, "your teacher is Poet Laureate of the whole United States."

I said, "I know," and showed him the invitation on the refrigerator. "It's a local celebration," I said. "They probably had the real ceremony somewhere in some big city."

"You're going, aren't you, Mom? You have to go," Evan said.

CHAPTER SEVEN

I was afraid to walk out the door. I didn't consider myself agoraphobic, because I did leave, quietly, grudgingly, and with great anxiety, whenever we ran out of something, (like food, soap, toothpaste, etc.) In fact, I would have preferred, like Norma Desmond or the old woman in Great Expectations, to linger in the luxury of my own home, as the ivy and wisteria covered the walls and the hedges grew higher and higher. If I'd been rich or famous, I'd have been allowed that wish. "She wants to be alone," they'd have said, "like Garbo." "She's reclusive," people would have whispered, "like Emerson or Thoreau."

I think too much of myself.

Chickens--they don't think much. They're always happy. The tiny chicks I'd purchased the year before were now big healthy hens. They had been part of a plan: I thought that if I planted fruit trees and a vegetable garden, and if I had my own free-ranging chickens, I'd never have to leave the house again, not even to go to the grocery store. (The chickens ate the vegetable garden, but we always have fresh eggs.)

I was wandering around the yard, hoping the fruit trees I'd planted had survived the frost, when I felt someone watching me. I turned to see Parker in an Adirondack chair, framed by a little grove of bare trees. Our eyes met, and I realized I wasn't looking at Parker...   I was looking at Amy. She smiled at me, lovingly.

I smiled. I felt happy for the first time in years.

Then the irises of Amy's eyes glowed magically, as if they were lit brightly from within. Maybe I should have been frightened, but instead I was enchanted.

CHAPTER EIGHT

The next day, when Evan showed up, we all sat in the living room. A football game was on TV. On the coffee table was a bag of candy. Parker ate a piece and tossed the wrapper to the cat. The cat kicked it around a minute and walked away. While Evan and I talked, Parker occupied the couch, drinking beer, eating fun-sized candy bars one after another, and tossing the little wrappers on the floor.

Evan stared at the wrappers. Then he looked at Parker.

Seemingly unaware that we were there, Parker punched the air furiously and yelled at the TV with a mouth full of candy.

I picked up the wrappers and Parker's beer bottles and went into the kitchen to make dinner.

Evan followed. "Need any help?" he asked.

I didn't, because the day before Parker had cheerfully made two dozen tiny pizzas and put them in the freezer. I took them out and put them on the counter.

Evan looked at the pizzas and nodded. "Nice," he said.

I preheated the oven.

Parker walked into the kitchen and said, "What're you doing?"

"I'm putting dinner in the oven."

Parker said, "Don't bother. I'm not hungry," grabbed

a beer, and disappeared into the other room.

Evan asked, "Where's the lady?"

"What lady?"

"The etiquette lady--where'd she go? I like her."

I sighed. "I like her too," I said. "She comes and goes. I don't know why."

Life went on that way for a few weeks. Then it was the day of the big reception. Parker and I looked and looked for something to wear. I finally decided on a tight black velvet turtleneck. I looked for a skirt to match, while Parker ironed a pair of pants. I felt nervous, as if I were on date. In fact, I'd felt that way a lot lately.

I put on a long black velvet skirt with a modest slit. I put on my black-rimmed glasses, (my only pair,) and dark red lipstick. I'd have worn a black beret and smoked a cigarette on a stick, if I'd had them.

"You look like a poet," Parker said.

I was satisfied that I'd achieved the look I wanted. Then I spoiled it all by putting on a big black coat, because it was a cold and foggy evening. "The tickets," I said. "We can't forget the tickets."

"Don't worry, I have them," The Ghost softly said.

I didn't want to step out the door that night, but I did. Parker drove, while I stared out the window and thought a lot of melancholy thoughts. All the way to the reception hall, I was nervous. Every writer or poet in town would be there tonight. Who was I, an unemployed waitress with a B.A. in English and an unfinished terminal degree? I was no one anyone would miss.

The dinner turned out to be fairly casual. Cocktail tables and chairs faced a young jazz band. Parker acquired two glasses of wine and led me to a table near the exit. We watched and listened to the music, while guests meandered into the hall. I saw a lot of people I used to know. They all looked the same. It seemed I was the only one who'd changed. I tried to think of the right thing to say to Levi Phillips, my esteemed teacher, who was hugging his old friends and politely signing autographs for strangers. He was a great teacher, generous and kind, yet tough at the same time. What I learned in his classes helped shape my life. I wanted to tell him that and thank him for all he taught me, but I didn't want to bother him.

Then I saw my old friend Emma Sherman, sitting in an out of the way place. Parker and I went and sat down next to her. I asked Emma how she'd been. She said, "I have terminal cancer."

She asked how I had been. I told her I hadn't gotten out much lately. My problems, compared to hers, seemed insignificant. We talked for a while. We said we'd get together soon.

People started making their way from the banquet hall to the auditorium.

"Maybe we should go find a seat for the reading," Emma said.

"Yes," Parker said.

We sat near the back of the auditorium. The Poet

Laureate was in the front row, along with a lot of people I used to know. One by one, colleagues and friends stood up to talk about Levi Phillips. They read from his books. Then the poet himself spoke, eloquently of course, and read some of his work. It was all very beautiful.

I cried. I don't know why. I kept silent, but I couldn't stop the tears. As I said before, I hadn't been out of the house for over a year, except for trips to the grocery store.

Parker handed me a Kleenex and whispered, "Are you okay?" but I knew it was someone else...Amy... She put her arm around my shoulder.

In the car on the way home, that beautiful woman's voice came out of Parker's mouth. "It will get easier. You've broken the grip of fear."

I said, "It was important. I had to go."

She said, "I know."

We slipped into a billowing patch of fog. I turned on the heater and turned up the radio. The song that was playing was "Haunted" by Poe.

That night, I dreamed I saw my father. I ran to him and hugged him and told him I loved him and how much I missed him. I said, "Rest in peace, Dad."

He said, "The dead don't rest. We don't get tired. We're trying to change the world."

Then I woke.

CHAPTER NINE

For the next few days, I spent a lot of time with Parker, who seemed, almost constantly, to be channeling the ghost of Amy Vanderbilt. See, usually, Parker sat on the couch all day, complaining loudly, while I made coasters, worked on my web site, and cleaned the house. Now, we were doing things together. We cooked. We baked pies for the neighbors. We made coasters. We listened to tunes. The ghost loved the B52s, and she liked to dance. We painted tiny paintings, and I listed them for sale online. We quit watching Jeopardy because Amy Vanderbilt knew all the answers. She loved to watch The Simpsons, (a show Parker never liked,) which was on at the same time. In the evening, we read books to each other by the fire.

Then I began to wonder if I had lost my mind. Perhaps I was so lonely and sad that I made up The Ghost to keep me company. Nobody wants to be crazy. Maybe, I thought, I have some control over the situation. I read somewhere, a long time ago, that if you tell a ghost to leave, it will depart.

Certain things are destined to fade into obscurity: workshop poems about waiting tables and old-fashioned phrases like, "How do you do?" Everything, even love, had come to seem impermanent to me then. I decided it was time to say goodbye to the ghost that had been keeping me company. I was tired of wondering whether or not I was crazy.

The next time Amy appeared in Parker's eyes, spouting her gentle phrases and her witty repartee, I said, "I'm not playing this Amy Vanderbilt game with you anymore. Just go away, and don't come back." Then I went into the bedroom to cry for a while, and I felt very lonely and regretful.

"What's wrong?" Parker asked, upon entering the bedroom to find me sitting in the dark, even gloomier than usual.

"I told the ghost to go away, and now she's gone," I cried.

"Why would you do that?" Parker asked.

"All those strange things going on... I began to think that I was schizophrenic."

"How can you be schizophrenic? For one thing, you're too old. That's a disease that strikes young people."

"Hmm," I said. "What about the ghost? What about objects moving by themselves?"

"I see them too—objects moving by themselves, lights that sparkle in midair," Parker said. "How can it be a delusion if I see it too?"

"Maybe we're both crazy," I said. "Anyway, The Ghost is gone, and I miss her."

"What makes you think she's gone?"

"I told her to go," I said, and I sobbed out loud.

Then Parker said, in a gentle tone, "Maybe you're not the boss of her," and laid a hand gently on my shoulder.

Nevertheless, I grieved. I kept to myself and moped and cried for days, as if I'd lost a friend I'd known for all of my sad lives. I tried hard to be normal, but instead I moved around like a zombie. I made coasters and listed them for sale. I straightened up the rooms. I cooked and cleaned. I did all the usual things, but it wasn't the same. I missed my ghost, with heart and soul. Her absence was something I could physically feel. In it, I had no doubt that she was real.

CHAPTER TEN

My ghost--she probably would not like to be called that. I should call her by the name she liked, Miss Amy Vanderbilt. Who knows, maybe she wasn't a ghost at all. I sometimes think she is an angel. Anyway, I missed her. I wrote her letters. I burned herbs and whispered her name. I was lost and hopeless without her. I felt resigned to loneliness forever.

Parker was back to his usual self.

I'm a morning person. I like the quiet of dawn. At six a.m. I was taking my first sip of morning coffee and checking my sales on the computer, when Parker came in and said, "We have to go to the bank. Why are you just sitting there?"

I said, "I just got up five minutes ago. I sold a set of coasters."

Parker said, "Oh great. Now we have to go to the bank *and* the post office. Where's your package? Why haven't you done it yet? I knew you'd drag your feet. I knew you'd mess this up. You should have done this yesterday."

"They paid at midnight last night," I said.

While I wrapped my coasters for shipping, Parker shouted that I was using too much tape, then not enough tape, too much paper, then not enough paper.

"Where are the packing peanuts?" he yelled. "We

need packing peanuts!"

"We don't have packing peanuts," I said. "It's okay. It doesn't matter. Professional packers use paper."

Parker didn't hear me. He was shouting, "I told you to save all packing peanuts. This is taking you too long. I thought you had a method. Why do those corners look so bad? I thought you had a plan for packing these things. I can't understand why this taking so long? It's only one set. This isn't worth it. I could do it faster. It wouldn't take this long if you used packing peanuts. You should have saved all packing peanuts. You should save them."

"I'm not saving them. I'm not using them. They annoy people," I said. "And they're not environmental."

"I can't believe you are taking this long," Parker said. "I want to get this in the mail. Why are you still in your pajamas?"

I got dressed while Parker said, "Hurry, let's get this over with. I think you're taking this long on purpose. You're dragging your feet on purpose. What's wrong with you?"

We got into the car and drove to the post office. It was closed. I looked through the window at the clock on the wall. It was seven-thirty a.m. We sat in the parking lot for half an hour. Then I mailed my package. Then we drove to the bank. The bank was closed. They didn't open until nine.

I didn't say a word all the way home. I thought my head was going to explode.

"How was I supposed to know? Parker said. "Now I'm going to have to hear about it all day. You're going to go on and on about how I messed up your morning." And then he uttered a long stream of expletives.

I stared out the car window and missed my ghost friend.

Parker was still yelling when we pulled into the driveway.

Later, I went into the kitchen, where Parker sat in the breakfast nook, reading the sports page. I said, "Would you like some apples and cheese?"

Parker said, "I don't want anything. I'm not hungry."

"Okay," I said. I, however, was hungry, so I got a knife, an apple and some cheese. I started to pare the apple.

Parker yelled at me, "What are you doing? I said I didn't want anything. Why'd you even ask me? I said I wasn't hungry. Don't you listen? There's something wrong with you. I'm not going to eat it. You're wasting food."

He stormed out of the room before I could say, "It's for me."

In the evening, I went into the living room where Parker was meticulously assembling a model trebuchet out of balsa wood. I said, "Dinner's ready."

Parker shouted, "Why didn't you tell me?"

"I just did," I said, bemused and irritated.

That night, lonely and sad, I sat in the white wingback chair and thought about the ghost. I was so sorry I had told her to go. I hoped she would forgive me and come back, but I doubted I'd ever see her again.

The next morning began like any other. Miss Hiss meowed at a quarter to six. I ignored the first meow. A few minutes later, she yowled. I ignored that too. Then she climbed up onto the bed, put her fuzzy mouth into my ear and howled at full volume. I jumped up, slipped into my slippers, staggered to the kitchen, and opened a can of cat food.

Parker came in right behind me, ground the coffee beans and put water in the machine. We stood and stared at the coffee maker and waited. As soon as possible, I poured two steaming black cups and mumbled "thank you" to Parker for making it.

Then I went into the living room and sat balled-up in my favorite chair, content. I was just sitting there, waiting for the fog to clear, listening for the old furnace to make its usual banging sound, several times in a row, before it hissed its heat into the white-breath dawn.

Parker walked into the living room, frowned, and said in a harsh tone, "What's wrong with you? What are you stewing about? Why are you sitting there, all enraged?"

"I'm not..." I said, quite honestly. (I was picturing bare trees on coasters.)

"Yes you are. Look at you. You're sitting there, all mad about something," Parker insisted.

"I'm not," I said.

"Yes you are. You're in a bad mood."

"What did I..." I tried to ask.

Parker pointed a crooked finger at me and said, "What are you so mad about? What did I do now? You're getting ready for a fight."

The irony struck me as funny, but I didn't laugh. I said, "Actually, I was thinking about..." I was going to say, "bare trees," but Parker interrupted...

"I can tell by the way you're acting that you just want to fight. Look at that expression on your face," Parker said, and he made a pouty face.. "When you have that look on your face, you want to fight.." Parker was wearing a sweatshirt that said "St. Mary's Alcoholic School." It once said "Catholic School," but I'd taken a big Sharpie pen to it, one bad night, and changed a couple of letters. Parker, unaware of this graffiti, now stood, leaning over me with a twisted, scary expression, applying this crazy-making tactic: asking questions and then yelling over my attempts to answer. "What's wrong with you? Why are you just sitting there? Shouldn't you be looking for a job? You think your stupid coasters are going to pay the bills? Are you just going to sit there all day?"

"I," I said.

"Why don't you call the Pumpkin Coach and get your old job back? Huh? Why don't you call the Pumpkin Coach? He handed me the phone. Call them right now."

I said, "It's six a.m. There's no one there..."

But Parker didn't hear me. He was saying, "Why are you just sitting there wallowing in self-pity? Why aren't you calling them? Poor Beth! Poor Beth!"

"Please stop yelling," I said.

Then Parker said, in a near-whisper, "I'm not yelling. You call this yelling? This is yelling, according to you. Is this what you call yelling?"

I said, "Oh my God. Here we go again. Parker, please leave. Just go somewhere and chill. I don't want to fight. I can't take it anymore."

"I am leaving you. I'm leaving next month," Parker said. "I've told you that a thousand times, so shut up about it."

"You've been saying "next month" for six years," I said. "Please. We need to make a plan."

Parker insisted, for the millionth time, that his plan was to wander the deserts of Arizona alone, with a mule, a miner's pick, a pan, a backpack, a little crank-powered radio...

When Parker stopped yelling to take a drink of coffee, I knew I had four seconds in which to speak. "Where is this desert full of precious stones, and are you allowed to camp there? What about scorpions, sunburns, and mirages? Do you want blistered lips? Where, in this country, is a person allowed to wander around, picking up gold and trinkets?" I asked, without pausing for any answers. (I learned this trick from Parker.) "You need a better plan than that. Call your cousins and ask if you can stay with them. They'd be happy to see you."

"Why do I have to leave? Why don't you have to leave?" Parker screamed.

"Because it's my house," I said. "I've lived here twenty years."

"Look at you," Parker said. "Look at the way you're acting. You're overboard. You're out of control."

"I'm not..."

"Yes you are," Parker pointed at me and yelled. "You're out of control. I knew you would act this way. I knew you just wanted to fight. I could tell by the way you were stewing."

"I wasn't..." I said.

"You were," Parker said.

"I didn't..." I said.

"You didn't have to do anything," Parker said. "I could tell just by the way you looked, the way you are sitting. You're mad about something. There goes the whole day. Look at you, just sitting there, pouting."

"I'm not pouting. I was feeling..." I tried to say.

Parker interrupted, "I know what you were feeling."

"I ..."

"You love to fight. It's all you love," Parker said.

"Me? I don't like to fight. I was just thinking about coasters."

"Yes you do. You love to fight. You're a hothead," Parker said. "You're mad about something, and you want to fight."

"You're the fighter," I said. "You do this to me all day every day. You do it to everyone. You fight with your friends. You even fight with your billion-year-old parents. I don't fight with anybody," I said, and I realized it was true.

Before Parker came along, I had never had a reason to fight. I don't think I'd ever yelled at anyone in my life, until I'd lived with Parker for some time. I even raised my son without raising my voice. Now I never seemed to have a moment's peace. I started crying. I couldn't help it.

Then Parker pointed at me and yelled at full volume, like a drill sergeant, "Look at you, crying like that. You're pathetic. What's wrong with you? There's something wrong with you. You know that? There's something wrong with you. I'm leaving you, and you're never going to see me again. Then what're you going to do? You're nothing but a..." Parker went on for a long time, calling me names, swearing like a sailor, telling me everything that was wrong with me, many times over, until I felt like my head would explode.

When I couldn't take it anymore, I burst out yelling. "You're bellicose and cruel. This whole relationship has been horrible. Will you please please leave?"

Parker was caught in a screaming loop, though, and didn't hear a word of it. "Look at you, crybaby. Boo hoo. Poor Beth. You're off the deep end. You've got problems."

"You're my problem," I said. "You make me feel this way."

"Then you should be happy that I'm leaving," Parker shouted. "I'm leaving next month. Do you hear me? Why aren't you happy? Why aren't you happy now that I'm leaving?" And then he taunted me and called me names a while longer.

I said, "Please get out of my house. Go out into the

desert with your imaginary mule. Please just leave. I'm begging you. I don't want to fight. I'd rather live alone with a ghost than fight with you all the time."

Parker went to the front door, unlocked it, and shouted. "I'm leaving you. You're never going to see me again. Ever! Don't try to find me either. I'm going to Arizona." Then he went and got his car keys from the desk drawer and went back to the front door. "I'm leaving you forever," he said. "I'm sick of you. You're never going to see me again. He called me names. "I'm leaving you forever," he said. Then he backed away from the door, flopped onto the couch and smugly said, "But not right now. Not this week, either."

"Please leave me alone," I said. The pain was starting in my chest. I was exhausted already, at seven in the morning.

"Make me," Parker dared.

I rushed at Parker, enraged. I don't know what I was going to do. As I lunged across the room, I saw a white spark fly through the air, as if racing me to my target. It shot right into the pupil of Parker's eye. Then someone else's countenance appeared on Parker's face. That person firmly but tenderly snatched my hand from the air, and very gently, pulled me down beside her on the couch. "Feel me," she said, holding my hand. She was very calm.

We were quiet for what felt like a long time.

Finally, I said, "Are you afraid of me?"

Amy only laughed and whispered, "No."

CHAPTER ELEVEN

That night, we went into the kitchen and made dinner.

When we were finished, "Parker" went to the sink to do the dishes, looked everything over with a squeamish frown and said, "There are a lot of greasy things here." She opened the cabinet, and took out a pair of rubber gloves.

"Would you like me to do those for you?" I asked.

"Oh, would you be so kind? I would appreciate it," was the reply, and it came with a sweet smile.

I jumped up and rushed to the sink.

Amy pulled up a chair, and as I cleaned, she read me poems, in that warm and lovely voice.

Even the suds seemed to sparkle that night. Standing there with my hands in dishwater and a stack of dirty pans on the counter, I was happy.

The next day, I decided to go shopping. I wanted very much to get my hands on more books by Amy Vanderbilt. I wanted to know everything about her. Parker was surprised but willing to go with me. We went downtown and walked around in the comfortable cold, under a soft gray blanket of clouds. Amy took my hand and said, "See, it's not so bad."

"What?"

"The world outside."

"Hmm," I said. I felt calm and hopeful. That strange and awful feeling was gone—the foreboding, the dark creepy feeling that something terrible would happen if I stepped out the door. And so we wandered through thrift stores and used bookstores. Then we went home.

We didn't find any of Amy Vanderbilt's books that day, so I went online and bought a used first edition cookbook, for a couple of bucks plus postage.

That night I lay in bed next to Parker, wondering, Why would someone like Amy Vanderbilt want to hang out with me? Was she slumming?

Parker was making out the grocery list.

I said, "Why does Amy Vanderbilt want to hang out in your body?"

"Because she's in love with you," Parker said, without hesitation.

I smiled, surprised. I said, "No, that's not it." I knew I wasn't worthy. My house has that "lived in" look. I'm dead weight at parties. I like to eat sandwiches over the sink--no plate--like a man. I wear mismatched socks. I complain a lot, and I'm boring. I could think of a million reasons for someone like Amy Vanderbilt not to be in love with me. Still, I lay awake that night, wishing it were true.

A couple days later, Parker was sweeping the porch, and I was outside watering, when the mail carrier stomped right past me and tried to hand Parker a package.

"Hello," I said. "That's my package. Thank you."

"What's inside?" she asked.

"A cookbook."

"Who is it? Rachel Ray? Paula Dean?"

"Amy Vanderbilt," I said.

"I've heard of her," she said, "Miss Manners."

"That's Judith Martin," I said.

"Yeah, she killed herself."

"Miss Manners is still alive," I said.

"Is that her book?" she said, pointing to my package.

"No, it's mine. I just bought it."

"Yeah, but who wrote it?"

"Amy Vanderbilt."

"I know who she was," she said. "She threw herself out a window and left a mess for other people to clean up."

"She did not," I said. I turned to go inside.

"Amy Vanderbilt, yeah, I remember. She killed herself and left a mess. How's that for etiquette?" she said again, and she cackled.

"She did not," I said. "She didn't kill herself. I know her. She wouldn't have done it." And I went back into the house, nearly closing the door on Parker, who was right behind me.

I went straight to my computer, and I googled Amy Vanderbilt. Suddenly, there she was, smiling, pouring coffee. She was lovely. I looked at another picture. The sight of her moved me deeply, mysteriously. I had to turn my head at first. Then I made myself look. Then I couldn't stop looking at her. She appeared exactly as I thought she would. I recognized the eyes. I'd seen them looking out from Parker's face a thousand times.

I clicked around online and read some brief biographies. According to sources, Amy had been dead for forty years. Most references listed suicide as the cause of Amy's death. I did not believe them. Her smile was just too bright. She didn't look depressed. I chose the photo I liked best. In this picture, Amy Vanderbilt is my age, and she looks pensive and very pretty. I saved it to my computer.

Parker walked up behind me, handed me a cup of coffee, and said, "Amy Vanderbilt?"

"That's her," I said.

"I pictured someone like Grace Kelly."

"She's beautiful," I said.

"I think you're beautiful," a warm voice breathed into my ear.

That night, Parker and I made dinner and dessert, meticulously following recipes from The Amy Vanderbilt Cookbook. The main course was "Delicate Sole." It was unbelievably good.

The lady seems to come and go at random. I often worry that she will get tired of me and leave me permanently. I'm afraid that if Parker leaves, Amy Vanderbilt will leave as well. She seems to fit nicely into Parker's body. If Parker leaves, where will that leave The

Ghost? I don't know. I've given up on asking Parker to leave. With Amy, I've found an awkward peace within a perfectly absurd situation.

The little spark still twinkles in the air. When she is not in Parker's body, she often hovers around the house, keeping me company. Lights flicker when I talk to her. Sometimes, objects move, as if touched by an invisible hand. I've grown accustomed to the magic, and I love my sweet companion. She has proven to possess a very rare blend of passion and self-restraint. Likewise, she is sensitive and sensible. She is also exceedingly smart.

I still don't understand why someone like Amy would want to spend time with me. I feel fortunate just to have her here. I'm trying to improve myself a little every day, so I might feel worthy of her company. I hope she never leaves me.

I've learned a lot about Amy Vanderbilt since then. To Amy Vanderbilt, etiquette was not an esoteric code for the aristocracy; it was a way of conducting ourselves in the nicest way possible. Promoting gentleness was her life's work.

Our life is still not perfect, but it's improving. For one thing, I'm no longer afraid to leave the house. I worry less about losing those I love. I have a sense of peace, now that I know that death is not the end. Perhaps the most important thing of all is this: I love and am loved, and that makes me happy.

Now, when Parker goes on a rampage, I just wait. Sooner or later, Miss Amy Vanderbilt appears in Parker's place. I usually recognize her immediately, but if I'm ever confused as to whom I'm speaking, I just hand Parker a hot coffee or a cold drink. Amy always uses a coaster.

ABOUT THE AUTHOR

Beth Webster's poetry, fiction, and artwork have been published in anthologies, periodicals, and some major textbooks. She was educated at California State University, Fresno. Her other books are *Ghosts Are Only Human, From the Files of Richard West, My Poems, and A California Fairy Tale, and Just for Fun, Let's Draw Cats.*